CHRISTIAN MOTHER GOOSE™

Un Petit Enfant Les Conduira™

#1 National Bestseller Author
MARJORIE AINSBOROUGH DECKER

is well-known and loved for her distinct story-telling style. Her CHRISTIAN MOTHER GOOSE™ CLASSICS have endeared the trust of parents and the twinkle of children across the world.

Softcover Edition ISBN 1-55748-008-7

Hardcover Edition ISBN 1-55748-009-5

Copyright © 1987 Marjorie Decker

Printed in the United States of America

P9-DNW-522

A child's faith is precious.
To live in faith is a journey.
When better to begin
the adventure
than when we are young!

FROM
CHRISTIAN MOTHER GOOSE™

This timeless *New* Collection from young believers' *Favorite Storyteller* is your Library to help little ones discover *Faith Adventures* for the entire family. Faith and Confidence Builders, Scriptural Truths, Fun-filled Allegory, Parables, Growth Enrichment . . . Encouragement and Biblical Principles abound!

CHRISTIAN MOTHER GOOSE® TALES

by
Marjorie Ainsborough Decker

Illustrated by

Theanna
Colleen Murphy Scott

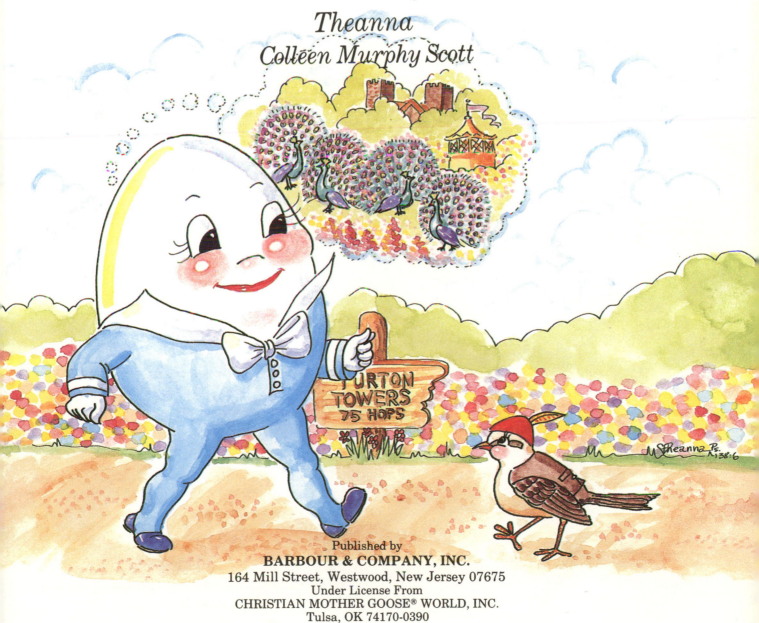

Published by
BARBOUR & COMPANY, INC.
164 Mill Street, Westwood, New Jersey 07675
Under License From
CHRISTIAN MOTHER GOOSE® WORLD, INC.
Tulsa, OK 74170-0390

WHERE DO ALL THE SOUNDS GO?

Oh, where do all the sounds go
   That have sounded out today?
Are they floating off to somewhere,
   Either near or far away?

The tiny, whispy whispers,
   And the loudest, loudest shout?
All the barks, meows and talking
   Filling up the air about?

The clucking and the chirping,
   All the merry songs around?
All the gonging and the bonging
   Rising up above the ground?

The words of men and women,
   All the roars and cheering noise?
All the laughter and the crying
   Of the little girls and boys?

Oh, where do all the sounds go?
   Will someday we see that place?
Where every word, and song and sound
   Is saved somewhere in space?

And though I cannot tell you
   Where the other sounds all go,
God has told me in the Bible
   Where our prayers go — Yes, I know
That the sound of little voices
   As they talk to Jesus, dear,
Fly quickly up to Heaven
   To His loving, listening ear!

TWO LITTLE HANDS

Two little hands
   Can hold Mommy's tight;
Two little hands
   Can send off a kite!
Two little hands
   Can hug Teddy Bear;
Two little hands
   Can show that they care.
Two little hands
   Can serve God each day;
Two little hands
   Can love Him and pray
Two little hands
   Can splash in a brook;
Two little hands
   Can open God's Book
Two little hands
   Though tender and small,
Are treasured by Jesus
   Best of all!

FARTHING SPARROW'S DISCOVERY

Humpty Dumpty was on his way to see the Peacock Parade at Turton Towers.

What a wonderful sight it was to see the Peacock family in their finest feathers; shining and glistening with all the colors of the rainbow. These handsome birds live in a summer house in the gardens of Turton Towers, and as Turton Towers is a fine mansion, you can well imagine what a lovely house the Peacock's enjoy.

"Not any cozier than my own little house by the wall, though," thought Humpty, as he strolled along, thinking of the Peacock's summer house.

Right in the middle of his thoughts, he met Farthing Sparrow coming down the pathway.

"You're going the wrong way, Farthing Sparrow," he said. "This is the day of the Peacock Parade, and it's a parade well worth your time and attention."

"I'm sure it is, Humpty," replied Farthing Sparrow, "but I have always felt I would be out of place in such fine-feathered company. After all, a little brown sparrow is not to be compared with the beautiful, stately, rich and confident peacock. Going there would only serve to make me more sorry about the Sparrow family tree."

"You are beautiful in your own way, Farthing Sparrow," said Humpty in a gentle voice. "It is written that God has made everything beautiful in its time."

"But look at my name — *Farthing Sparrow!* That means only half of a half of a penny! Sometimes I wonder if that is all I'm really worth — half of half of a penny. It's enough to make a sparrow feel quite undone . . . falling apart . . . and thoroughly discouraged if I think about it too long."

"Undone! Falling apart! Discouraged! Farthing Sparrow, don't even *say* those words. Let's sit on this rock while I remind you of some very special things today." Humpty's voice was very kind as he spoke to the little brown sparrow.

With his head hung down, Farthing Sparrow hopped upon Humpty Dumpty's soft knee to listen.

7

"Farthing Sparrow, you have wings! You can fly — fly through the clouds, hop over rooftops, watch the children swing from the best seat in the heavens. How much is that worth?"

"You are a home builder. You plan, build and finish the job for your family. And what's more, you are never in debt for any of your homes. How much is all that worth?"

"You can sing! And you've never charged anyone to listen. I've even heard you say that you can afford to give away your songs. So, in a way, that makes you a small phil-an-throp-ist." (That was such a long word, Humpty had to say it in little pieces.) "And to be a phil-an-throp-ist you have to be worth quite a lot!"

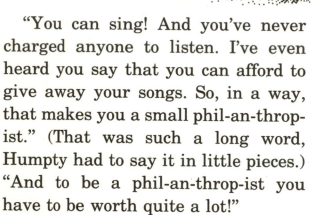

"You have personally carried thousands and thousands of seeds to fields that once were empty; and now they are rich in clover and heather. That makes you . . . pardon me, Farthing Sparrow, while I put this other long word together . . . that makes you an ag-ri-cul-tur-ist of the greatest degree. And to be an ag-ri-cul-tur-ist you have to be worth, oh, such a lot!"

8

"I say this with humility, and as modestly as I can: Farthing Sparrow, you live in the very highest of neighborhoods; in the most privileged of spots — right in the eaves of the House of the Lord! For centuries, it has been the talk of many bird gatherings, even among the Peacock family, that *your* family was welcomed in that precious house."

"Half of a half of a penny? That is your worth? Never! Farthing Sparrow, you are a bird with rich abilities — worth more than a small fortune."

By now Farthing Sparrow's chin was up, and his head was beginning to nod in agreement as Humpty Dumpty went on:

"It was actually written in God's great Book that the Sparrow family lived in His house! It is also recorded: 'Blessed are those who dwell in His house,' and that 'The blessing of the Lord maketh rich.'"

"You are rich, Farthing Sparrow!"

"And on top of all this, the Lord has also written that He is your guardian and the Champion of your fate. He watches over you and cares for you each day. That is worth more than all the world."

9

"Behold! a gentleman Sparrow . . . out of debt . . . self-employed . . . home-owner . . . flight expert . . . phil-an-throp-ist . . . ag-ri-cul-tur-ist . . . and above all — with a written guarantee that he is blessed of the Lord!"

"Ah, it is my great pleasure to accompany you today to the Peacock Parade."

"Will you kindly lead the way, Farthing Sparrow, Esquire." Humpty saluted in grand style, as the tiny sparrow hopped off his knee.

With his little head held high, and a big smile on his face, and with Humpty Dumpty taking little steps behind him, Farthing Sparrow led his own parade.

He felt perfectly altogether, and a bird of great worth.

And what's more . . .
His little brown sparrow heart was warm and happy . . . which was exactly as it should be.

SEVENTY TIMES SEVEN

Seventy times seven,
  Seventy times seven!
God's time table was
  Sent to us from heaven.

Why did Jesus tell us
  To remember every day,
Seventy times seven
  Time's table to obey?

Seventy times seven
  Are times we must forgive
Anyone, and everyone,
  As long as we live!

Forgiving on the left;
  Forgiving on the right;
Forgiving in the morning,
  Afternoon and night!

Seventy times seven,
  Our Father God knows best,
Will keep us all happy,
  Together and blest!

CHOOSING

My little house
    Has a green front door,
With a latch
    I can open or lock.
I can say, "Come in!"
    And open the door,
Or leave it shut
    When I hear a knock.

My little eyes
    Have a brown front door,
Which can close
    Or can open so wide
That I have to watch
    Which way it will swing,
As I choose
    What I bring inside!

My little ears
    Have a pink front door,
I leave open
    For most of the day;
And so many callers
    Like to drop in,
With a lot,
    Or a little to say!

My little mouth
    Has a red front door,
I can open
    Or keep it shut tight.
I can choose what goes
    In and out that door
With a few words,
    Tidy, and polite!

My little heart
    Has a white front door,
With a dear
    Little front door key.
And when Jesus knocked,
    I unlocked it quick!
Now He lives
    There inside with me!

GOD PLANNED HOUSES

God planned houses,
Houses by the score!
I just saw one
Along the seashore!
Sitting in the sun,
Like a nice hotel –
One little snail
In a house sea-shell!

God planned houses,
Hundreds, it would seem!
I just saw two
Propped up in a stream!
Sitting in the sun,
Tucked in tree hodge-podge –
Two little beavers
In a beaver lodge!

God planned houses,
Thousands in a day!
I just saw three
In a mound of hay!
Sitting, with a sign:
"Not Open Till Noon" –
Three butterflies
Asleep in their cocoon.

God planned houses,
More than ninety-three!
I just saw four
High up in a tree!
Sitting in the shade,
With room for some guests —
Four little birds in
Their own twiggy nests!

God planned houses,
Some to store and save;
I just saw five
In an old rock cave!
Sitting in the shade,
As the honey thrives —
Busy, working bees
In their five bee hives!

God planned houses,
One, a special one,
I just found out
Is for His dear Son!
Sitting up in Heaven
With rooms to spare —
Boys and girls who love Him
Will all live there!

FLUTES FOR SEVEN COUSIN MOLES

Grandpa Mole had made a secret present for each of the Cousin Moles . . . a beautiful, hand-made flute!

All over Dandelion Sea, Grandpa Mole was famous for the wonderful flutes he carved and polished. He was a master craftsman at his job.

For months, he had been quietly working on seven special designs.

Now and then, he would picture the little moles up on the bandstand in Polly Woggle Park, performing for the Petals and Praise Concerts each Saturday night.

The praise filled the air with music and song; and the petals filled the air with sweet perfume. Together, they made a lovely cloud to float up to the Lord.

Cousin Moles always sang with all their might at the concerts, but Grandpa Mole thought that learning to play the flute was now the next step for Noggin, Tilly, Mogie, Rimpy, Tolly, Dolly and Toggle Mole.

He had sent a special invitation to Cousin Moles. Charlie Cricket, who delivered the letter, was the only other one who knew what it was all about.

And now the flutes were ready and waiting!

Cousin Moles came bounding up the path to the tree house, just as Grandpa Mole's cuckoo clock cuckooed, "Two!" They looked their very best and had brought a present of their own . . . fresh peas from their pea patch.

"Sit around the table, little friends; close your eyes and then I'll bring in your presents," said Grandpa Mole in great excitement.

Of course, the Cousin Moles sat down very quickly, and shut their eyes till they couldn't see at all!

In front of each little mole, Grandpa Mole gently placed a beautiful, polished flute.

"Now you can look!", he chortled.

"Oh! Grandpa Mole! A flute! . . . A flute! . . . A flute!" All Cousin Moles filled the house with squeals and peals of happy wonder. But when Grandpa Mole raised his hands, they became quiet at once; as they felt that was the most grown-up thing to do when a Cousin Mole had a grown-up, hand-made flute.

"These are the best flutes I have ever made. And I am proud to give them to my dear little friends, the Cousin Moles!" said Grandpa Mole with much affection.

The Cousin Moles cheered to hear him.

"May we play them now?"

"There is no better time than the present to begin something worthwhile," Grandpa Mole assured them.

And that is all it took to make his tree house almost burst with funny music; as if a hundred birds were suddenly learning to sing!

"What are those strange sounds coming from Grandpa Mole's house?" Humpty Dumpty asked Benjamin Bumblebee, as they passed by.

But inside the tree house, Grandpa Mole sat basking in the squeaks and piping of seven Cousin Moles with their very first flutes.

With his eyes closed, all Grandpa Mole could see was his vision of admiring Dandelion Sea creatures, as they listened to Cousin Moles on the bandstand playing so beautifully . . .

"All things bright and beautiful,
All creatures great and small,
All things wise and wonderful,
The Lord God made them all."

HOW GOOD, HOW GOOD IS GOD!

A golden sun up in the sky;
How good, how good is God!
A hundred million stars on high;
How good, how good is God!
The falling rain to fill the streams;
How good, how good is God!
A silver moon with kindly beams;
How good, how good is God!

Rainbows of flowers and bushy trees;
How good, how good is God!
The singing birds and honey bees;
How good, how good is God!
The grassy fields and sea-shore sand;
How good, how good is God!
The wiggly things that sit and stand;
How good, how good is God!

18

The dancing breeze and juicy fruit;
  How good, how good is God!
The hills that wear a snowy suit;
  How good, how good is God!
A cozy house where we can live;
  How good, how good is God!
All good things He loves to give;
  How good, how good is God!

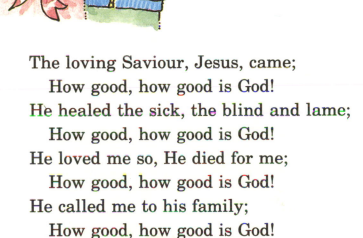

The loving Saviour, Jesus, came;
  How good, how good is God!
He healed the sick, the blind and lame;
  How good, how good is God!
He loved me so, He died for me;
  How good, how good is God!
He called me to his family;
  How good, how good is God!

He keeps me safe and cares for me;
  How good, how good is God!
Dear Jesus prays in Heaven for me;
  How good, how good is God!
He gave the Bible, so I know,
  How good, how good is God!
Oh, all His world and wonders show
  How good, how good is God!

TWO LITTLE CLOUDS

Two little clouds met together one day;
They smiled as they got into each other's way.
"Hello!" said the first cloud, "you look just like me";
The second cloud said, "We're alike! I agree."
The first cloud then asked, "Are you carrying rain?"
"I'm full to the brim," his new friend did explain.
"I noticed the fields down below look quite dry,"
The first cloud went on, "I don't want to pass by;
I'm not a big cloud, but I think, since we met,
Together we both could turn dry fields to wet!"

"I am rather tired of just drifting, it's true,"
The second cloud said, "and I'd like to join you
In blessing these fields, in the way God has planned,
And hear the glad shouts as we rain on this land."
His friend, the first cloud, said, "Together we'll drain —
When I count to three — every drop of our rain."
"One! Are you ready? Two! We're together!
Three! Rain away! Make the rainiest weather!"
And down came the rain; both clouds gave their best
Of splashing, sweet rain on their dry, thirsty guest!
The children ran out with their hands to the sky;
The little clouds smiled, and then said, "Goodbye!"

THE LOGOS-LEAF TREE

On the second Much-Merry Monday in May, Jane and Jonathan knocked on the door of Humpty Dumpty's little blue house. They were so excited that they jumped up and down as they knocked.

This was the day Humpty had promised to take them to see the Logos-Leaf Tree.

This wonderful tree is deep in the heart of the Rain Forest.

Humpty was ready to go the moment he heard the children knock on the door. He met them with a big smile. "Good morning, Jane and Jonathan. Sorrabahum!"

"Sorrabahum!" laughed Jonathan. "That's Grandpa Mole's saying."

"I know what it means," joined in Jane, "it means, 'Bless you, children.'"

"Right you are! And that's why I borrowed it from Grandpa Mole," chuckled Humpty. "I like what it means."

"Now let's start over the meadow to the River Dee. We'll wait there for the *Sharing Ship*."

"The *Sharing Ship*! We're going to ride on the *Sharing Ship*!" shouted the children together.

"Yes, it's a-sailing we will go," replied Humpty Dumpty.

So all three skipped down the pathway, and across the meadow to the River Dee.

Miss Muffet's house was on the other side of the river, and Webster, her butler, (don't ever call him a spider, will you?) could be seen polishing the golden bell on the front door.

The children waved to him, so Webster tinkled the bell to show how glad he was to see them again. He had served dinner to Jane and Jonathan, along with Christian Mother Goose, when they had visited Miss Muffet.

"Sing a song of sixpence,
A pocket for the LORD;
Four and twenty children
A penny could afford
To send across the ocean,
For other children there
To learn about dear Jesus,
Who answers every prayer!"

The Sharing Ship

In a few minutes, the "Toot-toot-toot" of the *Sharing Ship* could be heard; and around the bend it came. Charlie Cricket was at the wheel, and everyone aboard was singing. (When *you* ride the *Sharing Ship* you will want to sing, too.)

With a swish and a swash, Charlie stopped the ship alongside the bank. "Hurrah!" shouted all the other passengers, as Jane and Jonathan, with Humpty following, came aboard.

"Toot-toot!" went the horn, as Charlie set sail again. (It may be useful for you to know that two "toots" are for starting, and three "toots" are for stopping.) And right away, they all began to sing the *Sharing Ship* song again:

The ship sailed down the River Dee; past the town of Winkyville, then came to a stop at the bridge at Dandelion Sea. "Here is where we get off," said Humpty.

After the three "toots" to stop, and two "toots" to start again, the *Sharing Ship* chugged on its way once more, as Humpty and the children walked up the pathway which would take them to the Rain Forest.

Grandpa Mole's house is just halfway between the river and the Rain Forest. He had kindly invited the three travelers to stop at his house for lunch. This made the children hurry, and Humpty had to huff and puff to keep up with them.

In a short time, they had arrived at the tree house door. Grandpa Mole was waiting for them, and shouted out, "Sorrabahum!"

"Bless you too, Grandpa Mole," answered Jane and Jonathan. Humpty just smiled, as he was still huffing and puffing.

What a treat it was to have lunch in Grandpa Mole's interesting house. If you could have looked in the window, you would have seen the tasty bingleberry bread, fruit and nuts, and Grandpa Mole's own elderberry juice, so nicely prepared for his very special guests.

In less than one hour, lunch was over, and Grandpa Mole smiled his biggest smile when everyone hugged him as they said, "Goodbye."

24

Up the winding path went Humpty Dumpty, holding hands with Jane and Jonathan.

At last they came to Nothing-Impossible-Possum's house, where they stopped to rest a few minutes.

Nothing - Impossible - Possum is a well known Rainbow-Rain scout. He lives close by the Rain Forest to watch for signs of the Rainbow-Rain.

Humpty and the children were sitting under the great weather vane, when Nothing - Impossible - Possum leaned out of his window and shouted, "Welcome to the Rain Forest! I'm sure you must be off to your favorite tree, Humpty. And what a wonderful surprise is in store for the children there!" He knew that when Humpty made a special journey to the Rain Forest, it was always to see the Logos-Leaf Tree.

"Yes, I'm here with my little friends, Jane and Jonathan. This is a grand day for them to see the Logos-Leaf Tree," Humpty shouted back. "We'll be on our way again now. Good day." But Nothing-Impossible-Possum did not reply. He was peering closely through his telescope over the tops of the trees. After all, he *is* a Rainbow-Rain scout, and he must keep an eye on the clouds.

The children and Humpty soon reached Poetree Dale, which led them right into the beautiful and mysterious Rain Forest.

Jane and Jonathan gasped with delight at the wonderland around them. In all their days, they had never seen trees of such brilliant colors!

Every tree had a tint of color all its own. There was bright yellow, soft yellow, laughing pink and dainty pink, sky-blue, royal blue, deep lilac and pale lilac; rosy-red, orange-red, grass-green and forest-green; and all sorts of colors the children couldn't name!

Jane and Jonathan kept spinning around like spinning tops, trying to see everything at once, and shouting, "Oo – oo – oo!" They were lost for words. But Humpty Dumpty knows the language of children well, and he quite understood all they were trying to say in "Oo – oo – oo!"

"Now, children, we're going into the very heart of these trees, to the Logos-Leaf Tree. It is surrounded by Redhood trees, Perch Birch, O'Pinion trees, Sleeping Pillow, and other curious, colorful trees. But the Logos-Leaf Tree remains the only one of its kind in all of Christian Mother Goose Land. Take my hand and we'll go together," Humpty said. So hand in hand, the three good friends walked excitedly to the very center of the Rain Forest.

"There it is!" shouted Humpty, as he pointed to the biggest tree of all. The children raced ahead to be the first there. They held onto the trunk of the giant tree, staring upwards with all their might, wondering . . . wondering.

Humpty soon reached them, puffing just a little. "Why is it different than all the other trees?" Jane asked.

"It grows all the colors of every other tree here," noticed Jonathan.

"Ah! that's true", answered Humpty, "but that's not the reason it's the only one of its kind."

"Please tell us right away," Jane begged.

"First we must lift up Jonathan to bend a branch down, so that we can examine it closely," said Humpty, as he held Jonathan high to catch the nearest branch.

"Carefully, now, with the branch, my boy," he said, as he let Jonathan gently down. "I'll hold the branch while you both look at it, very, very closely."

With eyes wide open, the children looked over, under, and all around the branch; oh! so closely! But they saw nothing other than lovely colors.

"Please give us a hint, Humpty. We don't see anything at all," they sighed.

"Well . . . the clue is in the leaves. Look again," smiled Humpty, still holding the branch.

Jane suddenly squealed with delight! "I see it, I see it!" she cried. "Look, Jonathan . . . a letter . . . right in the leaf."

Jonathan put his face as close as Jane's to the leaf. "It's an *O*!" he shouted in surprise. And so it was! A perfect *O* in the veins of the leaf.

"Look at this one! It's an *E*." Jane happily jumped as she found more and more letters.

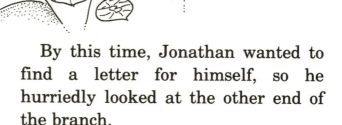

By this time, Jonathan wanted to find a letter for himself, so he hurriedly looked at the other end of the branch.

"Jane! Here's a *G*, and an *L* . . . there must be all the letters of the alphabet here!"

"Yes, you're quite right," laughed Humpty. "The whole alphabet is here. Every leaf contains a letter. That's why it's called the Logos-Leaf Tree. Logos means "word", and there are words all over this great tree."

28

"But I only see letters, and letters have to come together to make words," said Jonathan, with a puzzled look.

"A very good point, my friend," replied Humpty. "So let me explain. As you can see, these Logos leaves are growing nicely all over this tree. But to make words, they must come together in a special order; each letter in the right place. And that is the secret of the Logos-Leaf Tree. It knows the right order, and it knows the right words. Some words are more important than others, you see. Watch, children, as we let the branch go."

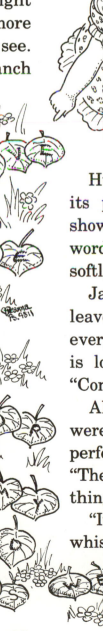

Humpty let the branch fly back to its place, and down came a little shower of rainbow leaves. "Read the words, now, little scholars," he said softly.

Jane looked down at the lovely leaves around her. Words were everywhere, as plain as could be. "God is love", said nine leaves together. "Come unto Me", said another group.

All around Humpty and Jonathan were other leaves with their letters perfectly in order. "I am the Door" . . . "The Lord is my Shepherd" . . . "All things were made by Him".

"It's a tree that tells us about God," whispered Jonathan.

29

"Always . . . always," nodded Humpty. "You'll find the whole world is full of things which tell us about God. But the best leaves of all are the leaves in the pages of God's own Book. He has put all the words together in the right order, to tell us how much He loves each and everyone."

"We are learning from God's Book everyday," said Jane.

"And we'll always remember what we learned here today, Humpty. We will . . . we will," promised Jonathan.

"Well, little friends, it is now time to leave, so that we can catch the *Sharing Ship* to take us back home."

Humpty took Jane and Jonathan by the hand as they walked back through the Rain Forest. They didn't see the Logos-Leaf Tree gently drop a few leaves behind them as they left. The leaves read: "A little child shall lead them."

THE "TOGETHER UMBRELLA"

Little Lucy Ladybug was carrying her violin to the Petals and Praise concert at Polly Woggle Park.

She had practised a song all week, and hummed it as she walked along:

> Praise the Lord . . .
> Little tiny things!
> Praise the Lord . . .
> Mountains, hills and kings!
> Praise the Lord . . .
> Wind and rain and snow!
> Praise the Lord . . .
> Everywhere we go!

Just as she reached the pea patch, where Cousin Moles live, it began to rain.

Little Lucy quickly tried to cover the violin with her flower dress, but the raindrops splashed on the bottom just the same.

"Oh dear," she began to cry, "my lovely violin will get all wet."

Just as she said those words, a big umbrella was raised above her head to nicely cover both Lucy and the precious violin.

Holding onto the umbrella was Brother Rabbit.

"I'm on my way to Polly Woggle Park, too, Little Lucy. Let's stand by this bush till the shower blows over."

Little Lucy Ladybug felt snug and safe to be in from the rain under the big, red umbrella. There was plenty of room to even play a song while she waited with Brother Rabbit. So she made one up just to fit the occasion:

"Umbrellas can bring us together
    As the rain comes falling down;
So we don't mind if the weather
    Puts on a smile or a frown.
'Together' is always nice to be;
    I am with you and you are with me!
Umbrellas can bring us together
    As the rain comes falling down."

"What a fine song, Little Lucy," beamed Brother Rabbit. "I've never thought of my umbrella quite that way before."

"From now on, I think I'll call it my 'Together Umbrella'."

"Shall we start walking to the concert now? And let's sing your song as we go."

So off they went under the "Together Umbrella", singing all the way through the pea patch. And as quickly as it had started, the rain stopped.

But Brother Rabbit and Little Lucy Ladybug enjoyed their togetherness so much, that they left the "Together Umbrella" up all the way to Polly Woggle Park.

PITTER, PATTER BLESSING

If you want to be
    Where God commands
The blessing,
    Then you must stand
All together!
    If you want to be
Where God commands
    The blessing,
Then you must love
    One another!

If you want to bring
    Sweet pleasure
To the Lord,
    Then you must stand
All together!
    If you want the world
To know about
    His love,
Then you must love
    One another!

Pitter, patter, blessing!
Pitter, patter, blessing!
Where God's children
Stand together;
Pitter, patter, blessing!
Pitter, patter, blessing!
When God's children
Love each other.

THE WIG-WAGGY PATH

There's a Wig-Waggy Path
   At the edge of town,
And it leads to the valley
   Down below;
It begins at a fork
   In the road, where two signs
Point the way
   For the travelers, as they go.

It happened, one fine day,
   Cousins Moles reached the fork,
As they rode with a basket
   Full of flutes.
They were off on their way
   Helping dear Grandpa Mole,
When they saw the signs
   Which showed different routes.

Grandpa Mole had told them,
   "Take the sign that says 'Straight',
When you ride with the flutes
   To Dingley Tide.
It won't take very long
   To reach the music shop,
With the flutes I've made
   With hand-crafted pride."

With Noggin at the front,
   And Toggle at the back,
Cousins Moles had stopped
   To take a short rest.
They looked off to the right,
   And looked off to the left,
To decide on the way
   They thought was the best.

34

On the Wig-Waggy Path
　　Pretty flowers grew tall,
So it didn't take them long
　　To decide
That the Wig-Waggy Path
　　Was the prettiest one,
And must lead in the end
　　To Dingley Tide!

"Hurray! and off we go
　　Down the Wig-Waggy Path!"
All the Cousin Moles
　　Were happy to agree.
Noggin, Tilly, Mogie,
　　Rimpy, Tolly, too,
With Dolly, and with Toggle,
　　Fancy free!

The flowers by the path
　　Very soon disappeared;
And prickly thistles
　　Sprouted up instead!
As the Wig-Waggy Path
　　Took them down, down and down;
Through bends
　　And waggy branches overhead.

The moles got thirsty-dry,
　　And stopped to get a drink
At a fountain
　　In a mossy-green glen.
The fountain, too, was dry,
　　So all the little moles
Stayed, oh! so thirsty
　　As they rode again.

Down deeper on the path,
    They came across a house
Where a man looked out
    A small windowpane.
"Please may we have a drink?"
    Noggin asked, as they stopped;
"We're thirsty, sir,"
    He started to explain.

"Oh, I never go out
    In the rain," said the man,
As he shouted
    Through the small windowpane;
"I might get soaking wet,
    And I might catch a cold;
No, I never will go out
    In the rain."

"But it isn't raining,
    Is it?", said Cousin Moles.
"But it *might*,
    And it's *dangerous* going out!
See all those clouds up there?
    They could rain anytime,
Then you'll get a drink of water,
    There's no doubt."

The thirsty moles rode on,
    Down the Wig-Waggy path,
To a house with some black sheep
    They heard bleat.
The man inside the house
    Said he never comes out,
As he might meet a lion
    In the street!

Tilly, Tolly, Dolly,
    Had tears upon their cheeks;
"We're so thirsty,
    No one cares," they cried;
"And the Wig-Waggy path
    Keeps twisting down and down;
How will we ever get
    To Dingley Tide?"

The boy moles now looked sad,
    So they stopped on the path,
And prayed someone would come
    To help them there.
They looked up hopefully,
    Believing in their hearts:
"Little moles can see
    An answer to their prayer."

36

Up the Wig-Waggy Path
　　A kindly man appeared,
With a cane,
　　And a water bottle, too.
"I can't believe my eyes!"
　　He shouted in surprise,
"A cycle full of moles!
　　How do you do?"

"Are you an angel, sir?"
　　Whispered all Cousin Moles;
"Will you save us from
　　This dry, thirsty state?"
The kindly traveler smiled:
　　"An angel, I am not!
I *was* the Crooked Man,
　　But now I'm straight!"

"I used to live down here,
　　Down the Wig-Waggy Path,
And I walked a crooked mile
　　Every day;
But since I read a Book where
　　God makes the crooked straight,
They call me Mr. Straight,
　　The Water-way!"

"You see, I know the ways
　　Of the Wig-Waggy Path,
And this air will make you
　　Thirsty, and so dry.
So I come here every day
　　To see who needs my help;
And I always bring
　　A nice, fresh drink supply."

"A drink! A drink! A drink!"
　　Cousin Moles danced about,
As they drank sweet water
　　Up to their fill.
"Now, Little Moles, turn back
　　Up the Wig-Waggy path,
And I'll help you
　　Reach the top of the hill."

So Cousin Moles returned
　　Up the Wig-Waggy Path,
With Mr. Straight
　　Assisting at their side.
At last they reached the top,
　　And the fork in the road,
And took the Straight Path
　　Quick! to Dingley Tide!

GOD SAID . . .

God said . . . "Light be!"
At once the light was there!
God said . . . "Water!"
And water did appear.

God said . . . "Land, sun,
With moon and stars, now be!"
Straightway they were there,
In shining finery!

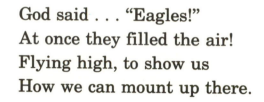

God said . . . "Eagles!"
At once they filled the air!
Flying high, to show us
How we can mount up there.

God said . . . "Peace Doves!"
So gentle is their name,
He chose one to alight on Jesus
As the Spirit came.

God said . . . "Penguins!"
(I'm glad He wanted those!)
Here they came a-waddling
In their black and white clothes.

God said . . . "Goldfish!"
They answered, "Here we are!"
(I think He knew, some day I'd
Need a few in my jar.)

God said . . . "Apples!"
And apple trees appeared!
They came with seeds in apples,
To grow trees for years and years.

God said . . . "Wheat-grain!"
And right away it grew!
Turning into loaves of bread
For boys and girls like you!

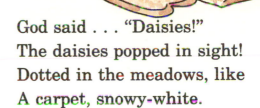

God said . . . "Daisies!"
The daisies popped in sight!
Dotted in the meadows, like
A carpet, snowy-white.

God said . . . "Fireflies!"
At once they came, so bright!
With lamps for tails, to light up
As they fly in the night!

God said . . . "Puppies!"
And there they were with tails!
Ready for a-wagging, like
Some friendly little sails.

God said . . . "Children!
And let them be like Me!"
Oh! I am *glad* He said so —
That's how *I* came to be!

WHO EVER THOUGHT!

Who ever thought,
That feather by feather,
God could put birds
Together, together!

Who ever thought
That by speaking some words,
God could made sky
To hold all of the birds!

BUTTERFLIES AND BUZZING BEES

Butterflies and buzzing bees,
Dandelions dancing in the breeze;
   Little orchids,
   Purple, yellow flowers everywhere!
They all seem to tell me
That God really cares!

Little flowers are full of grace,
Happy with the sun upon their face;
   They just gently grow
   And shed their fragrance everywhere!
They all seem to tell me
That God really cares!

THE TENDERTUFF PLANT

Grandpa Mole and Christian Mother Goose were enjoying an afternoon of bird-watching — and bird listening!

Chickadees were whistling at their best; the wood thrush would sing no less than a full concert; after which the wrens would pipe: "Cheery, cheery, cheery."

Not to be left out, the woodpeckers would drum, "Wick-a-wack, wick-a-wack, wick-a-wack!" And whenever there was a moment's silence, the mockingbirds would imitate all the others.

"The time of the singing of birds is come," laughed Christian Mother Goose.

Grandpa Mole nodded in agreement as he swept his telescope around the countryside. "That's a strange sight," he mused, fixing his gaze across Cousin Moles' pea patch.

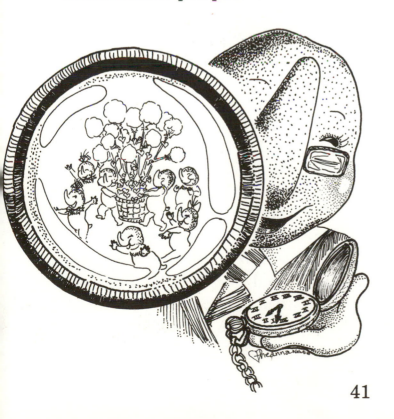

"A new bird?" asked Christian Mother Goose eagerly.

"No, but I do say it's a new sight for Cousin Moles. Look at their antics!"

Noggin and Toggle were holding a giant plant, while the rest of Cousin Moles ran around them in great excitement.

"That's the first one they've ever seen," chuckled Grandpa Mole. "And I vouch those little moles will be here within two minutes to ask us about it." He took out his pocket watch to check the time.

41

In less than two minutes, Tilly, Tolly, Dolly, Mogie, and Rimpy were running and jumping around Christian Mother Goose, while Noggin and Toggle stood proudly holding the giant plant.

"What is it? What is it?" they kept shouting.

"We've never seen one of these before!"

"We found it in the pea patch today."

"If everyone will sit down, we'll tell you about it," Grandpa Mole promised.

Immediately, all Cousin Moles sat down, as quiet as could be.

"This is a most unusual plant, and the only one of it s kind. A long time ago, Christian Mother Goose and I learned a wonderful story about it."

"Tell them the story, Grandpa Mole," urged Christian Mother Goose.

The little moles drew close around the storyteller as he began:

42

"Off in the valley of Bethgali-Buff,
     Grows the mysterious plant, Tendertuff!
The Tendertuff plant is remarkable stuff;
     Its wonderful tales can't be told oft enough.

Some say it began as a single, small seed;
     Nobody noticed; and no one gave heed;
Till one sunny day, on a dry, barren bluff,
     Appeared the white wonder they call "Tendertuff".

So soft and gentle, it looked to the eye,
     As if it would blow with the wind to the sky.
The town called it "Tender" — and tried with a puff
     To blow it away; but Tender was tough!

So, Tendertuff then was its lasting name;
　And in a short time it had gained much fame.
I'll tell just a few of the tales and the ways
　That Tendertuff won all the villagers' praise.

It happened one year, as the Tendertuff spread,
　The harvest was short, and there wasn't much bread;
Till someone discovered a secret so sweet —
　That Tendertuff seeds were exactly like wheat!

Thousands and thousands of starry seed pods
　Poured out their seeds with the touch of a rod.
Laughing and shouting came each neighborhood:
　"Taste of the Tendertuff seeds, Oh how good!"

When water was scarce from the shortage of rain,
　The Tendertuff stems were all found to contain
Gallons of water, so fresh to the taste
　That everyone filled up their barrels with haste.

44

Soon all of the children were laid down to rest
   On soft downy pillows of Tendertuff's best
Feathery tips, of the whitest of white,
   Which gave them the nicest of sleep every night.

The children all know it's a mystery deep,
   How Tendertuff always lights up when they sleep.
So now all the children as they go to bed,
   Will carry a Tendertuff candle, instead!

They love its sweet smell, and they love its soft glow,
   As they kneel to thank God for loving them so.
"God bless dear Mommy and Daddy," and then
The Tendertuff nods as each child says, "Amen."

There's really no end to the blessings you'll find
   In the Tendertuff plant; it's one of a kind!
Yet from one small seed, I've good news to report:
   That Tendertuff's spreading by land and seaport.

No weather or soil in the worst of condition
   Can stop Tendertuff from its kind, healing mission.
It takes root wherever a crack lets it in;
   Then Tendertuff blessings sprout up and begin. . .

45

Growing in gardens, and growing in streets;
Growing in winter, and in summer heat;
Growing in mountains, and dry, sandy plains;
Growing in forests, and by country lanes;
Growing in meadows, and growing in rocks;
Growing in plant-pots by grandfather clocks!
Growing in castles, and cottages small;
Growing on fences, and over a wall!
Growing in North, and the South, East and West;
Growing to bless the whole world as its guest;
Growing in baskets, and growing in carts;
But best of all – Tendertuff's growing in hearts! "

46

BARNACLE BEN AND BARNACLE BESS

Nothing-Impossible-Possum one day,
    Found two crusty barnacles sunk in dismay.
They sat all alone on the River Dee sand,
    Shaking their heads, as they sat hand-in-hand.

"What can I do for you, as a new friend?
    You look as if everything reached a sad end.
I'm Nothing-Impossible-Possum," said 'NIP',
    "I gather you're waiting to catch the next ship?"

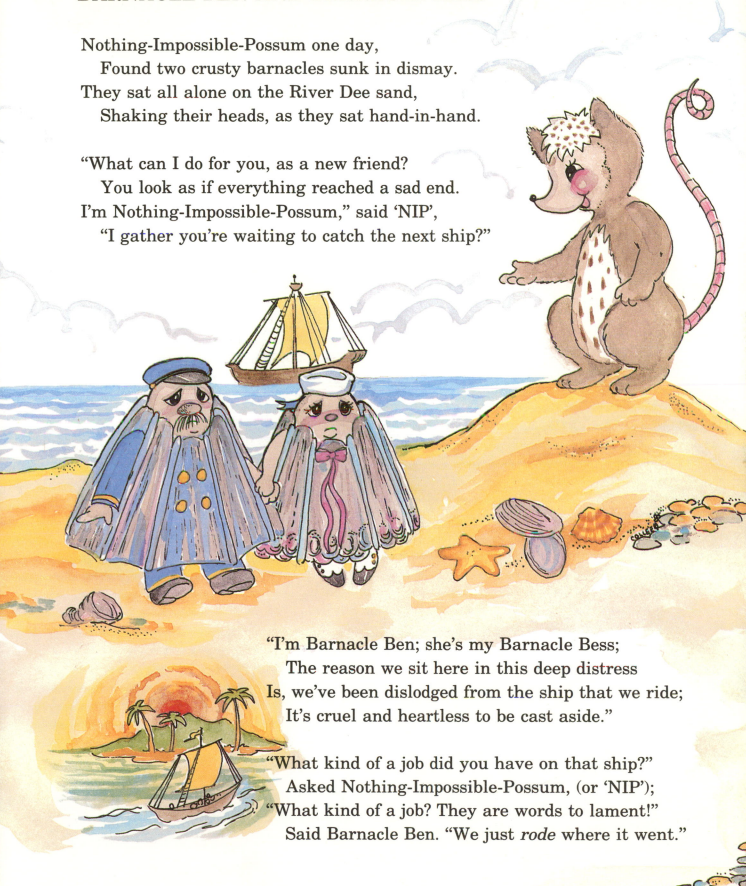

"I'm Barnacle Ben; she's my Barnacle Bess;
    The reason we sit here in this deep distress
Is, we've been dislodged from the ship that we ride;
    It's cruel and heartless to be cast aside."

"What kind of a job did you have on that ship?"
    Asked Nothing-Impossible-Possum, (or 'NIP');
"What kind of a job? They are words to lament!"
    Said Barnacle Ben. "We just *rode* where it went."

"We clung to the bottom, without any fuss;
    We never made trouble; no one noticed us;
We have no ambition for so-called success;
    We went where the ship went," said Barnacle Bess.

"That's true," said her partner, old Barnacle Ben,
    "We rode anywhere that it took us, and then
We never complained if it went east or west,
    But trusted the ship to do what it does best."

"You've made no decisions at all in your life!
    Concerning direction for you and your wife?
My, my this is time for this positive NIP,
    To get you to think other things than a ship!"

"A barnacle riding won't gather much moss;
    There must be a way you can be your own boss;
It's never too late, Ben, to get a new grip,"
    Said Nothing-Impossible-Possum, (or 'NIP').

"You think at *our* age, we can get a new grip
    On more than the bottom of some moving ship?
I tremble to think of the strain and the stress
    Such change would impose on my Barnacle Bess!"

"Dear Barnacle Ben, this is time to confess
    My feelings were hurt," said his Barnacle Bess;
The day they dislodged us, I heard the ship's mate
    Say you and I both were a crusty dead-weight!"

48

"*Now*! That makes a difference," said Barnacle Ben;
  "Dead-weight, did they say? Well, we'll not ride again
On any such thing as an ungrateful ship;
  I've made up my mind. We *will* get a new grip!"

"To make up your mind, that's the first step to do,
  To start a new life full of challenge for you!
A positive barnacle soon can equip
  His dreams," said the Nothing-Impossible-NIP.

"Our dreams, did you say?" whispered Barnacle Bess,
  "For years, as we drifted, I had to suppress
A deep, hidden longing that plagued me inside:
  'How nice to buy tickets, and *choose* where to ride'."

"Then here is Step Two, to that dream's satisfaction;
  We'll back up Step One with some definite action!
I know that the lighthouse on Cockle-Bay strip,
  Is looking for help," said the positive NIP.

"I do believe, dear, this has worked out for good,"
  Said Barnacle Ben, and Bess quite understood.
"Then off to the lighthouse I'll guide you," said NIP,
  "And this will be different than riding a ship!"

So, Barnacle Ben with his Barnacle Bess,
 Held hands as they walked in a new hopefulness.
At first, they were fearful to choose their own way,
 But NIP kept encouraging them to the Bay.

The old lighthouse keeper said,"Fortunate me!
 A barnacle has much experience at sea,
And knows all the ways of a sea-faring ship;
 What fine lighthouse keepers they'll make, Mr. NIP!"

And now when you see Cockle-Bay's light at night,
 It's Barnacle Ben who earns keep, keeping light!
Instead of just clinging below on a trip,
 It's Barnacle Ben who's now guiding the ship!

And Barnacle Bess? Well, her dream *did* come true;
 They now buy a ticket, and cruise with a view!
They've even sent gifts to the town's Sharing Ship;
 Three cheers for the Nothing-Impossible-NIP!

50

EBENEZER EAGLE'S WART

Ebenezer Eagle woke up feeling very sad. A wart had been growing on his beak for some time, and now he could no longer ignore it.

And more alarming still, he was sure the wart was the reason for some strange things that had been happening to him lately.

When he tried to land on a high, narrow ledge in the cliffs, he kept missing the mark and losing his balance. This was cause for great concern to an eagle who could see a speck a mile away, and swoop down upon that speck in a flash, because he knew it was really a tasty bit of dinner.

As Ebenezer thought about his amazing flying feats, it brought back memories of wonderful days.

"I have expert balance; and I'm more graceful than a trapeze artist at flying, swooping and gliding high," he comforted himself. "Well, I *used* to be an expert at that sort of thing," he slowly admitted to himself.

His head drooped forlornly. "Miles into the air with freedom and power . . . that was you . . . yes, *you*, Ebenezer Eagle. Riding high above the storms whenever you wanted to. Oh, they were glorious days . . . I wonder if they are over?"

He raised his head to look up in the sky; "King of birds, that's what they called me. It really was a very nice title to own."

"I wonder if anyone else has noticed my clumsiness? In all my years it never once crossed my mind that I would get into such an awkward state. There must be something wrong; and the only 'something' that I can see is this wart on my beak."

Ebenezer then looked over the edge of his cliff home. For the first time since he was a very little eaglet, he felt frightened, and timid. The valley *did* look so very far down below.

"I don't think I will try any difficult flights today. But now that I think about it, it never used to be difficult to land on a thin strip of rock overhanging the cliffs. Yet I've missed that ledge for weeks, and wobbled off a number of times. Where has my balance gone?"

At that moment, a young eagle went soaring by; a beautiful sight for any bird to see, let alone a fellow eagle who knew what it was like to fly with strong wings, and ride the wind as a fearless companion.

"There's no wart on *your* beak, brother eagle, of that I'm sure," said Ebenezer. "I wonder if all eagles find a wart on their beak one day or another? Am I old enough for such a thing to happen to me? No, not at all," he answered himself. "I see eagles older than I am, flying as perfectly as that young one who just went by."

Now that he had said those words, Ebenezer's head drooped lower down still.

"I think it will be best if I sit in a cave somewhere. It will be less embarrassing, for one thing; and perhaps I can study my situation seriously, for another. I'd rather not see any of my friends for a while . . . there would be too much explaining to do. But really . . . how can I explain when I don't even know myself what my trouble is? Yes, for certain, I shouldn't see anyone at all."

So Ebenezer set out to look for the best, most secret cave where he could hide for . . . well, he wasn't quite sure how long.

He walked carefully along craggy paths in his cliff mountain. He had never walked for very long before. His marvelous wings were his favorite way of getting from place to place.

"I must say, this is a different sensation, walking so far. But at least I am learning how other creatures feel who only have legs." Ebenezer kept talking to himself. It seemed to him to be the most helpful thing to do.

"Walking and talking . . . talking and walking . . . be a walking, talking eagle, Ebenezer, for now, anyway."

"Oh dear, but I am really a high-flying, fear-defying eagle! Yes, indeed, that is *really* what I am! I well remember my mother telling me so, as she nudged me out of the nest for the very first time."

"What a fearful sight awaited me that day! The edge of the cliff; the valley so far, far down below; but mother's great wings were above me as she kept moving me to the edge of our mountain home. How I wanted to be back in the soft down of our big nest! How could I know what to expect? A little eaglet who had never flown before?"

"Ah, but I can still hear mother singing her song as she jostled little Ebenezer Eagle off into the air for his first flight. Hmmm . . . a song can be such a help when you aren't sure what is going to happen to you. And since I could be mistaken for a walking, talking eagle, I think I should sing that song again to remind me that I am *really* a high-flying, fear-defying eagle! "

Then down the craggy pathway, leading down towards the valley, Ebenezer Eagle began to sing the song he had heard so long ago:

"Out of the nest,
   Shoo, shoo, shoo!
Mother knows best
   What eaglets should do!
Don't fear the fall,
   Don't fear the shove;
Trust mother's wings,
   Trust in her love.
     Little wings soon
      Will learn to fly,
     Lifting my eaglet
      Up in the sky.
     High-flying, fear-defying
      Eaglet, that's you!
     Ebenezer Eagle,
      Shoo, shoo, shoo!"

"And I did fly! My wings worked wonderfully well . . . after a few times of practice, and mother catching me."

By now, Ebenezer's legs were getting tired. He had walked quite a long way down the rough mountainside. He was still looking for the perfect cave to hide in. As he rounded a bend, the beautiful sight of a waterfall greeted him.

The waterfall made such pleasant sounds that Ebenezer stopped talking to himself and stood still, to listen to the water instead. He let the water splash on his face; and he even smiled. Then he felt the wart on his beak again, and the smile left.

55

Looking very sad, he perched on a cool rock. And then he saw the cave! It was almost hidden by a big bush and part of the waterfall. It was the perfect place he had been searching for.

With weary legs, Ebenezer crept into the cave. It was cool, and not too dark inside. He was thankful for that, and perched near the entrance, where he could see sunbeams sparkling through the flowing edges of the waterfall. In a little while, he fell asleep.

When he woke up, he was hungry, but he was afraid to leave the cave. As an eagle, he was used to hunting for his meals in the daytime, and sleeping on a safe perch near his great nest.

"Even my daily habits are all mixed up, and I'm more than sure it's this wart on my beak that's upsetting everything about me," mumbled Ebenezer in the heart of the cave.

Then he heard the sound of young boys singing. He trembled as he listened.

"I shouldn't have come down the mountainside this far," he barely whispered. "But then . . . this *is* the perfect cave for me." So he quietly crept to the farthest corner, and forgot about his hunger as he listened to the strange sound of boys' voices so close by. The song wafted into the cave:

"They that wait upon the Lord
   Shall renew their strength,
They shall mount up
   With wings as eagles!
They shall run and not be weary,
   They shall walk and not faint,
Mount up, mount up,
   Like the eagle!"

"Eagle! They said, 'eagle'," Ebenezer told himself. He was so happy to hear that word that he stopped trembling.

"Humans can mount up like eagles? I wonder how? Oh yes! They *did* sing, 'They that wait upon The *Lord* shall renew their strength!' "

Then in the softest of whispers he said, "Oh Lord, if humans can find new strength by waiting on You, can You renew *my* strength as I sit here waiting in this cave? Then I could mount up again like eagles; because I *really am* an eagle! Just as You made me."

He could still hear the boys singing, as they faded away in the distance, but Ebenezer sat very still . . . waiting.

After a few moments, he turned his head in the dark corner, and felt a very sharp rock. He rubbed his beak against it; testing it. And just as if a light had shone into his mind, he knew at once what an eagle with a wart on his nose should do.

And he knew, too, that such a thought was a high-flying, fear-defying true eagle thought! "Rub the wart against the sharp rock. Grind it off; clean it off; rub, rub, rub until it's gone! Start now, Ebenezer!"

He didn't wait any longer. He started rubbing his beak against the rock. The rock was strong, and Ebenezer was glad of that. Little by little, he could feel the wart wearing down.

Now and again he would stop, step out of the cave and wash in the splashes of the waterfall. Then back to the sharp rock he would go, to keep on cleaning his beak.

Layer by layer, he gradually cleaned away every trace of the troublesome wart. How clean and finely polished his beak felt. Even the sides of his mouth were improved from the polishing.

"I was right to come into this rock cave; I *know* I was right." He felt comforted and thankful.

"I wonder how long I've been here?" By now, he couldn't tell how long he had been in the cave.

After one last washing in the waterfall, he sat in the sun to dry. He loved to face the sun and feel its warmth all over. The sun was shining on his high, cliff home, so he knew it was now morning time.

The new Ebenezer sat up, straight and proud, as eagles should, then looked back at the rock cave.

"Can I mount up again, now, Lord?" he asked eagerly.

And as if in answer, a strong swirling of wind gathered about him. "I can! I know I can!" shouted Ebenezer, with trembling and excitement all mixed together.

The wind grew stronger about him, and with a great cry, Ebenezer rose up on the wind . . . higher and higher. The wart was gone, and so was the clumsiness!

He soared up past his high cliff home; turned on the wind, then sailed down to land on the narrow rock ledge. He landed expertly; a better landing than he had ever done before. His balance was perfect!

Oh, what joy! Back into the air he rose again . . . King of birds, diving faster than any eagle he ever knew! Down through the air he plunged in a dazzling display. As he passed the rock cave he cried out loudly, "Ebenezer Eagle! High-flying, fear-defying! Thank You!" The wind whistled with him as he rose again.

The boys in the valley watched in wonder the glorious flight of Ebenezer Eagle, as he soared off into the sun.

LITTLE SHIP

Little ship, I set your sail
　To follow with the winds of God
The course of life The Son of God
　Has laid for you, today.

Little ship, I place aboard　　　　　Little ship, the flag you fly
　Your compass and your sacred chart:　　Flies bravely o'er the waves below;
God's Word to guide your tender heart　It bears the Name of Jesus, so
　From sea to sea, each day.　　　　　Your course is safe in Him.

Little ship, sail on, sail on;
　Bring home a cargo, rich and true,
To Him Who gives the Light and Life to you
　To sail; sail on!

Little ship . . .
　Little ship . . .
　　Sail with God!

60

EVERY LITTLE TREE

Every little tree
   Waving merrily,
Sings that "God made me!"
   Happy as can be!
Every little creature sings —
   Ladybugs and leaping frogs
And tiny things with wings.
   All around the world,
Happy songs unfurled,
   Floating up above,
Telling of God's love;
   Singing, singing
One big song:
   "I'm so happy
God loves even me!"

THE UN-TANGLING CAN

To begin a fine day
In the finest of way,
There is nothing much handier than
A smooth-soothe-out device,
To keep everything nice;
Yes, I have one! An Un-Tangling Can!

Now an Un-Tangling Can
Has a spout that can span
All the way from right here to up there!
So the tangles you meet,
In your house, field or street,
Can be fixed and smoothed out anywhere!

In my can is a balm,
With a perfume to calm
Any squabble or tangled-up mess;
And its rich, creamy oil
In a flash can uncoil
Twisted tangles, with ease and success!

I can untangle horns,
Even those with sharp thorns,
And I untangle them in quick style;
I can untangle rope,
Tied in knots without hope,
And rewind it in neatly stacked pile!

When my pal, Porcupine,
Wore a coat made of twine,
And then found he could not get undressed;
He just called for the man
With the Un-Tangling Can,
To unravel his problem's request!

When a rabbit named Jack,
Thought he'd mastered the knack
Of the high-jump across a tall fence;
But one day missed his mark,
And got stuck in the bark,
I retrieved him with little expense!

Once, the Weasel twins tried
To get both heads inside
Of a tempting, half-full stewing pan;
When they couldn't get out,
I just popped in a spout
Full of oil from my Un-Tangling Can!

I am glad to report,
Twisted words, long and short,
Have untangled, and calmly smoothed out
In a wonderful way,
As I gave them a spray
Through my Un-Tangling Can's friendly spout!

So with horns and with thorns,
And with rope without hope,
And with rabbits with habits that stick;
With stuck-tight weasel twins,
And with porcupines' pins,
They can all be untangled, so quick!
But with words you have heard
That have hurt, be alert!
Be determined to stand like a man!
Till they're all straightened out
With the oil from the spout
Of your very own Un-Tangling Can!

64

TO FLY OR NOT TO FLY?

Poor Benjamin Bumblebee,
They said he couldn't fly;
"He's much too roly-poly
To lift into the sky.
Hopping might just fit him;
He might learn by-and-by
To jump into the air — but,
He'll never, never fly!"

Poor Benjamin Bumblebee,
Would make no quick reply,
But whispered down inside him,
"As God made me, so am I!
See here — He gave me wings;
And wings fly! — I can't deny;
My roly-poly bumble
On my wings it must rely."

While everyone still argued
The pro's and con's of why,
*"Poor Benjamin will never,
Oh! never reach the sky,"*
Benjamin buzzed his wings,
Shouting loudly, *"Yes, I'll try!"*
Straight off he flew his roly-
Poly bumble to the sky!

UPSTREAM, DOWNSTREAM

The sun was tip-toeing over the top of the Mustard Mountains as Nothing-Impossible-Possum stopped along the river bank to examine a Compass Plant.

Travelers in the Mustard Mountains find the Compass Plant a friendly guide. Its upper leaves always point north and south the minute they are touched by sunshine.

"Yes, I'm going in the right direction," said Nothing-Impossible-Possum to his very own self.

"Follow this river bank upstream, keep going north, and then I should reach the Crystal Caves."

Thinking of the Crystal Caves and what they might hold, made him happy. And as he had just reached a steep hill, it was an especially good time to think happy thoughts.

Climbing up the hill, he sang a song between huffs and puffs. He made it up as he went along:

"Upstream, upstream,
Yes! we're going upstream;
Never fear, we'll get there!
Yes! we're going upstream!"

Nothing-Impossible-Possum liked the sound of the new song, and only had to sing it five times before he reached the top of the hill.

66

"Now that I'm on top, I can easily run down," he told himself. With bounding and leaping, he laughed all the way to the bottom of the hill.

His knapsack of food bumped up and down on his back as he ran. "Breakfast, breakfast, now it's time for breakfast," it seemed to say as it thumped and bumped.

"Thank you for reminding me, knapsack. And here's a nice grassy spot waiting for me to set a table."

Nothing-Impossible-Possum is fond of sitting at a table to eat, so the first thing he unpacked from the knapsack was a little linen cloth. When he spread it out on the grass, he had his own table in an instant. Four smooth rocks were handy to hold down each corner.

As he unpacked apples, mushrooms, nuts and brown bread, he began another song:

"He prepares a table for me,
A table for me,
A table for me;
He prepares a table for me
Up in the Mustard Mountains."

67

"Not a table, not a table, not a table," the gurgling river seemed to shout as it rushed by.

"Not a table! Of course this is a table," the little possum shouted back.

"Has no legs, has no legs, has no legs," the river gurgled on.

It's not the *legs* that make a table. It's the *top* that counts. Four legs without a top? Now that is *not* a table; but a *top* without legs — that *still* can be a table." Not worrying about the river's remarks anymore, Nothing-Impossible-Possum went back to his singing.

By now, the sun was very warm, and strolling brightly across the Mustard Mountains.

"It's a good time for breakfast," the cheerful traveler decided, and closed his eyes to pray.

"Plop, swish! Plop, swish!" The sound of a rowing paddle made him look up as soon as he had said, "Amen."

Paddling hard upstream came Cobblecut the cobbler; the smallest of the five cobblers who live at the foot of Mustard Mountains.

Cobblecut spied the white cloth right away, and pulled over to the bank.

"Good morning, Nip," he shouted.

(Nothing - Impossible - Possum doesn't mind at all being called "Nip" by his friends.)

"Hello, there, Cobblecut! Come and join me for breakfast, and tell me where you're off to."

Cobblecut got out of the log canoe and sat down at the legless table. "I'm on my way to Timberwind with tools and leather. They want to start a cobbler's 'Good News' shoe shop up there, and I'm going to teach them the trade."

The little cobbler and possum talked of good things as they shared breakfast together in the warm sunshine.

As they finished, Cobblecut asked, "Now . . . where are you going, Nip?"

"I'm going up to the Crystal Caves to look for relics of the Tool-makers and the Tale-makers. They lived on these mountains many years ago, and I hear the Crystal Caves hold some of their secrets."

"Well, without a doubt, Nothing-Impossible-Possum is the very one to find such things," said Cobblecut, with a twinkle in his eye. "I'd be happy to give you a ride upstream, and save you some walking. The Crystal Caves are close to Timberwind."

"Thank you, Cobblecut. I'll help you paddle up the river."

So without any more delay, Possum folded his cloth back into the knapsack.

Cobblecut took his place in the front of the boat. "You make yourself comfortable in the back, Nip," he said. The bags of tools and leather filled the rest of the canoe.

"Plop, swish! Plop, swish!" They were soon paddling upstream and enjoying the sound of the paddles as they pushed along.

"It's not easy going upstream," Cobblecut observed. "I'm glad that you're here to help."

Suddenly, a blue jay screeching in the sky caught their attention. "Danger, danger! The river is flooding!" the blue jay kept shrieking.

"Hold on, Cobblecut!" shouted Nothing-Impossible-Possum, as rushing waters tumbled around the bend. How frightening it was as the river raced down to engulf the little log canoe. It was all the struggling friends could do to hold on to their paddles.

This way and that way, the boat was tossed, but Cobblecut and Nip pushed as hard as they could against the strong waves.

Then from the back of the heaving canoe Nothing-Impossible-Possum began to sing:

"Upstream, upstream,
Yes! we're going upstream!
Never fear, we'll get there;
Yes! we're going upstream!"

He shouted louder as the waters crashed against them, "Sing, Cobblecut! This is the song of the hour!"

And between gulps of river water getting in their mouths, and paddling hard to keep their canoe pointed upstream, they kept on singing, "Upstream, upstream, Yes! we're going upstream!"

70

No sooner had Possum said those words when another great surge of water raced down upon them. It was filled with little rafts and logs bobbing down with the rushing waves.

All sorts of little creatures were holding on to the rafts. They shouted as they sailed passed the brave log canoe:

"Downstream, downstream,
Yes! we're going downstream;
On we go, with the flow,
Easy-sailing downstream!"

"Upstream, upstream!" two voices kept on singing, as four small arms kept pushing with all their might against the swirling river.

Struggling to keep his place in the canoe, Nothing-Impossible-Possum's mind remembered what he had learned from a Tale-maker's story Grandpa Mole had told him... "When you pass through the waters, I will be with you; and through the rivers, they shall not overflow you..." Oh, what courage those words gave him! And what added strength!

"Upstream, upstream,
Yes! we're going upstream!
Thank You, Lord,
You're aboard,
Yes! we're going upstream!"

Cobblecut caught the new words right away, and took extra courage, too, as he sang along.

And through it all, the little log canoe kept her nose pointed upstream!

Right then, huge wings swept above them. It was Christian Mother Goose!

She landed on a bank nearby and called across the river, "Keep on keeping on! The waters are slowing down ahead of you. It was a flash flood. The worst is over. Bravo! You'll soon reach your goal!" Then off she flew again.

At the sound of those cheering words, the Beaver family popped up out of the waters. They cheered the little boat, too, as it still struggled on.

The big waves soon began to sink lower and lower. Cobblecut and Nothing-Impossible-Possum were now too tired to sing anymore. But their paddles went "Plop, swish! Plop, swish!" again as they reached kinder waters.

At last they came in sight of the Crystal Caves. They felt like heroes; soaking wet; with arms that ached; but the knapsack and bags of tools and leather were still safe in the canoe.

"Let's lie down on the bank to dry out and take a rest," sighed Cobblecut, as they moored the canoe.

"I can't wait," agreed Nip.

Stretched out on the grassy bank, the two little friends soon fell fast asleep. Cobblecut snored. Nothing-Impossible-Possum kept murmuring in his sleep, "Upstream, upstream. Yes! we're going upstream!" as he dreamed of what he would find in the Crystal Caves . . .

But that's another story!

THE BREAKFAST THAT GREW!

At seven o'clock in the morning,
   Humpty Dumpty had started to cook
His last two eggs for his breakfast,
   When a little voice spoke: "Stop and look!"

"*Two* eggs for yourself, Mr. Humpty?"
   The little voice spoke deep inside;
"Wouldn't *one* egg, with toast and honey,
   Be enough to be satisfied?"

"There's little Tom Tucker, your neighbor,
   Who might like a poached egg today;
Let's give him that speckled one, Humpty;
   Please take it to him right away!"

So Humpty skipped down to the hedgerows
   Where Tom picked wild berries each day;
Humpty said, "Here's an egg, Tom, for breakfast,
   You can add to your berries today."

Tom smiled as he watched Humpty Dumpty
   Skip back to his house, oh, so spry!
"My breakfast is growing," Tom chuckled;
   Then noticed Boy Blue passing by.

Boy Blue looked so tired and weary,
   From hours of rounding up sheep,
That Tom quickly gave him the breakfast,
   To take home and, "Get a good sleep."

74

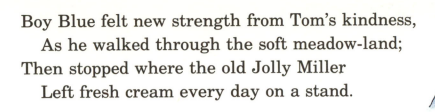

Boy Blue felt new strength from Tom's kindness,
　　As he walked through the soft meadow-land;
Then stopped where the old Jolly Miller
　　Left fresh cream every day on a stand.

"Fresh cream, scrambled egg, and some berries
　　For breakfast, then sleep once again,"
He said as he crossed the river bridge,
　　Meeting Hickety Pickety Hen.

Hickety Pickety's basket of eggs
　　Was heaped past the top of the rim,
"I sold not *one egg* yesterday," she said,
　　Tucking six in his basket for him!

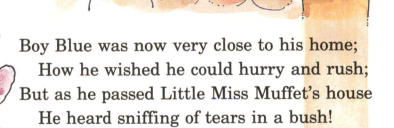

Boy Blue was now very close to his home;
　　How he wished he could hurry and rush;
But as he passed Little Miss Muffet's house
　　He heard sniffing of tears in a bush!

He looked underneath all the lilacs,
　　And there, hidden off in the shade,
Was Webster, Miss Muffet's dear butler,
　　Mopping tears with a napkin brigade.

"Oh, dear," sobbed the sad little butler,
　　"I've ruined my good butler's name."
Boy Blue asked him kindly, "Now, tell me,
　　Whatever has caused such a shame?"

"Oh, Boy Blue, as I went on an errand,
  To purchase some eggs yesterday,
I was hurrying to Hickety Pickety's,
  When I saw some good soccer in play."

"The Tittlemice versus the Dormice,
  Were brilliant! And played fair and square!
At the end I rushed over to Hickety's,
  But she'd closed, with a minute to spare."

"Now, I've no egg for Miss Muffet's breakfast,
  And till now, she could always depend
On my service." His gloves were so tear-soaked.
  "Many thanks for your listening, my friend."

Boy Blue said, "Come out; cheer up, Webster,
  And put on a clean pair of gloves.
Here's a basket of breakfast to cover
  Your good name, which our neighborhood *loves*!"

"Oh, thank you, Boy Blue; how I thank you!"
  Webster ran to the house to prepare
A poached egg, golden toast, and some lilacs
  To dress up the breakfast with flair!

"You are so dependable, Webster,"
  Miss Muffet remarked. "By the way,
I've crafted a present for Humpty,
  We can take with some lunch for today."

"Will berries and cream, and some nice fresh eggs,
  With lilacs, be suitable, Miss?"
"Oh, Webster, you're perfect," Miss Muffet smiled,
  "And your basket deserves a nice kiss."

76

Miss Muffet took Humpty the basket,
   With her present on top with a bow;
She had cross-stitched a lovely wall-hanging
   With a verse she hoped Humpty would know.

"This basket looks quite like Tom Tucker's"
   Humpty quietly said in his heart;
"Boy Blue's cream? Speckled egg with five others?
   Have all gathered from so far apart?"

As Humpty unrolled his new present,
   He read what was cross-stitched in blue,
And thought of the little "Give" voice inside,
   And what it had told him to do.

Give and it shall be given unto you, good measure, pressed down, shaken together, running over...

He thought of his friends who had listened
   To their little "Give" voice, as well;
And wondered what blessings *they* would receive,
   And what stories they'd all have to tell!"

As he hung up the lovely wall-hanging,
   With a "Thank you," to Miss Muffet, too,
He said, with his eyes all a-twinkle,
   "Have you heard of The Breakfast That Grew?"

"I know all about the beginning,
   And I know all about it's good end;
But when I know the middle, Miss Muffet,
   I will tell the whole story, my friend!"

MY SECRET

I heard that little children
    Came to Jesus, day by day;
And that He loved to touch them
    As He walked along the way.
Although He had His Father's work
    To do upon this earth,
I think I know another
    Special reason for His birth!

I know the Bible tells me
    That He loved me so, He came
To save me, and to keep me
    In His lovely Saviour Name!
But shall I tell my secret?
    Would you like to know it, too?
(I'm sure it's quite alright with God,
    Because I found He knew!)

My very own dear secret,
    Children all can understand,
Is that Jesus came to earth
    To touch the children with His hand!
He touched them! Yes, He touched them!
    And He held them on His knee;
Oh! He couldn't wait to come
    To earth to say, "Come unto Me!"

GROWING!

I'm just a little tortoise;
  Slow . . . slow . . . slow .
But I *do* have places to
  Go . . . go . . . go .
You ask me how I'll go there? I'll
  Show . . show . . . show .
One step at a time on each
  Tip . . . tip . . . toe!

I'm just a little fellow,
  Slow . . . slow . . . slow .
But to be like Jesus, I'll
  Grow . . . grow . . . grow .
You ask me how I'll grow so? I'll
  Show . . . show . . . show .
One step at a time on each
  Tip . . . tip . . . toe!

EARTH'S INVITATION

"Come! Plant your seeds!"
    Said the earth one day;
It's spring! I'm waiting!
    Bring what you may!
My larder is full
    Of life to give
To seeds and roots,
    If they'll come to live
In my nice warm house,
    Which I've prepared
With joyful bounty
    All to be shared.

The Lord Himself
    Commanded my rest;
Now I'm ready
    To welcome each guest!
I'll groom each one
    With loving care,
Each with a special
    Wardrobe to wear!
I have no lecture
    To give each seed;
Only my strength
    To fulfill its need.

80

Come now! Come today!
 In sweet springtime;
Just this one thing
 I request: Since I'm
Opening the door
 Of my generous sod,
Please offer thanks
 To the Lord, our God;
For even the earth
 Is nourished by prayer,
And I will be blessed
 With harvests to share!

THE TOMORROW CATCHERS

Once upon a sunny Dandelion Sea day, Grandpa Mole and Cousin Moles . . . yes, all of them . . . Tilly, Tolly, Dolly, Toggle, Noggin, Mogie and Rimpy, met together in the field behind Grandpa Mole's tree house.

They were launching off on an exciting journey. Grandpa Mole's balloon and a friendly wind were waiting to take them to the castle of the Tomorrow Catchers!

Cousins Moles didn't know what to expect when they got there, but all the little moles felt very safe, and knew they would learn wonderful things whenever Grandpa Mole took them on a journey in his balloon.

"One, two, three, four, five, six, seven . . . seven Cousin Moles all safely in the basket," Grandpa Mole called out. Stretching his hands across their heads, he thanked the Lord for a safe journey. At once, the friendly wind lifted them up, high above the tree house.

Brother Rabbit and Bo-Peep ran out to wish them, "Happy Sailing!" Benjamin Bumblebee buzzed his wings from the tip-top of the tree house.

82

Charlie Cricket, who was delivering letters down Leafy Lane, saw them flying, and shouted, "Do you have the *Today Book*?"

"Yes, we have the *Today Book*," Toggle Mole shouted back. Toggle knew they had it, because he had to stand on it to keep it in place.

"Does *everyone* know where we're going, Grandpa Mole?" asked Tilly.

"It seems as if everyone in Dandelion Sea must know," laughed Grandpa Mole.

In fact, nearly everyone *did* know. It had been the talk of the town for over a week that Cousin Moles were going with Grandpa Mole to the Tomorrow Catchers' Castle.

Once in a while a weather balloon, sent off from the Tomorrow Catchers, would float down into Dandelion Sea. Clusters of villagers would gather to examine it. Everyone wondered what kind of people the Tomorrow Catchers were.

Grandpa Mole was the best one to find out! And Cousin Moles were so proud that he wanted them to go with him . . . although they were not quite sure why.

"Little moles think different things than bigger moles, sometimes," said Noggin, "and I think that's why Grandpa Mole brought us along."

"Why are they called Tomorrow Catchers?" asked Mogie.

"I don't know," replied Noggin.

"Are we Tomorrow creatures?" asked Dolly.

"No, moles are Today creatures, I think," answered Noggin.

"What is the difference between Today and Tomorrow creatures?" Dolly chattered on.

"I don't know. Ask Toggle, he's standing on the *Today Book*," Noggin said with a sigh.

"We can't read it while I'm standing on it," Toggle reminded them.

"It's Grandpa Mole's book, and he knows all about it," Tolly nodded. "He said it's very important, and that's why he brought it today."

"Cushaw! Cushaw." The balloon rose higher. Grandpa Mole looked through his telescope. They were passing over Christian Mother Goose's house. Very quickly they left most of Christian Mother Goose Land behind them.

Cousin Moles kept squeaking and shouting as they saw new sights down below them.

They sailed over some chipmunks who were having a picnic.

"Look at the basket of moles up there!" one of them cried out.

"Moles are supposed to be in holes, not in balloons," another chipmunk answered.

Rimpy cupped his hands around his mouth and shouted down, "We're going to the Tomorrow Catchers' Castle!"

The chipmunks stopped eating. They were shocked. "They must be brave moles," they said to one another.

When Cousin Moles heard that remark, they smiled big, brave smiles at each other. The balloon sailed on over hills and deep valleys.

Watching carefully through his telescope, Grandpa Mole suddenly shouted, "There's the castle!".

The little moles became very quiet, as each one peered over the edge of the basket to catch sight of the Tomorrow Catcher's Castle.

"Cushaw! Cushaw!", the balloon began to ease down in a field close to the gates of the stone castle. The countryside around them seemed very, very still.

Grandpa Mole lifted each Cousin Mole out of the basket, then took the big *Today Book* under his arm. "Follow me, and stay together," he reminded them.

So Cousin Moles lined up behind him, just the way they do on their long sepcycle, with Noggin in front and Toggle at the back. They followed obediently to the big iron gate.

The gate was open, and for the very first time, little creatures from Dandelion Sea walked up to the door of the Tomorrow Catchers' Castle.

Grandpa Mole lifted the huge door knocker and banged three times. All Cousin Moles stood behind him, very close, and held their breath.

The great wooden door swung open, and a curly-bearded face peeped at them in surprise.

"Good day, sir," Grandpa Mole greeted him, in an extra friendly fashion. "I'm Matthew Mole from Dandelion Sea, and I've come with Cousin Moles to bring you a gift."

"A gift? Come in, if you please, do come in."

85

The curly-bearded man led them into a large, stone banquet hall. Four other curly-beards were sitting around a long table, studying old, big books.

"Five Curly-Beards live here!" thought Grandpa Mole, as Curly-Beard One introduced them:

"This is the Mole family from Dandelion Sea. I thought it would save time if they met us all at once."

Curly-Beard Two looked up and said, "We'll call you 'Mr. Mole' and 'Little Moles', so that we won't have to waste time remembering your names."

"Of course, of course, of course," said Curly-Beard Three.

"We haven't told him our names yet," whispered Tolly to Dolly.

"Then how can he forget to remember what he doesn't know?" Dolly whispered back.

"Perhaps it has something to do with being a Tomorrow Catcher," hinted Tilly.

"We need all the time we can get for the study of catching tomorrow," said Curly-Beard Four.

"Yes, we keep our minds set on that goal of catching tomorrow," said Curly-Beard Five.

"Catching tomorrow?" asked Noggin slowly. He was standing underneath the *Today Book* that Grandpa Mole was holding, and felt safe to speak from there.

"It's gratifying to see little moles interested in such a deep study as 'tomorrow'," murmured Curly-Beard Four.

"You are the first moles ever to come through our gates," mumbled Curly-Beard Five as he thumbed through a yellowed, old book.

Curly-Beard One beckoned them to sit down.

The table was almost as long as the room, and there were plenty of chairs all around it, but Cousin Moles crowded all together on one side. Grandpa Mole took the empty chair at one end of the table. He placed the *Today Book* in front of him.

"Ah! You seem to have brought some important literature with you, Mr. Mole," said Curly-Beard Two.

"Undoubtedly, it deals with the subject of Tomorrow?" inquired Curly-Beard Four.

"Quite the contrary," answered Grandpa Mole, trying hard to remember some of his very best words. "It is called the *Today Book*."

"Today!" All five Tomorrow Catchers closed their big books with a bang! Dust flew everywhere.

Curly-Beard Five stood up. "Mr. Mole, look above you."

Grandpa Mole, along with all the Cousin Moles, strained his head back as far as it could go to look all around the high walls.

For the first time, they saw a row of giant butterfly nets hanging across the top of each wall. They looked like rows of still flags, with brightly colored banners attached to each one.

"Those are the nets of honor from former Tomorrow Catchers," Curly-Beard Five continued. "Households who spent their lives in the pursuit of tomorrow. As all creatures should know, time has wings; and time flies! So we have made the finest butterfly nets, and built the best hourglass in the land, so that we can see the last grain of sand at that magic moment when tomorrow flys by."

87

"We have only that one moment in which to catch tomorrow," said Curly-Beard One, solemnly. "And we prepare every day in the hope of catching it. Our task is difficult, as we must try each night to catch Tomorrow in the dark. You may stay and watch if you wish."

Cousin Moles all breathed out, "Oh . . ." in one sound. The thought of staying up late, and watching Tomorrow Catchers, almost took their breath away.

"We have little time for eating and resting, Mr. Mole, but you will find simple food in the cushion room. You may rest there till midnight." Then leading all the moles, Curly-Beard One took them upstairs to a room full of cushions.

Grandpa Mole shared the simple food between them.

"Please don't forget to wake us up, will you, Grandpa Mole?" asked the Cousin Moles sleepily.

Grandpa Mole nodded. And Cousin Moles fell fast asleep.

At a quarter to twelve, the Tomorrow Catchers knocked on the door. Try as he would, Grandpa Mole could not wake up even one little mole. They were snuggled in the cushions, with just their noses sticking out, and he knew they wouldn't wake up till morning.

Grandpa Mole quietly followed the Tomorrow Catchers to the roof of the castle. A balcony surrounded it. Tiny bits of moonlight helped him see better in the dark.

The biggest hourglass he had ever seen stood on a pedestal. Only a little sand was left in the top, as it slowly trickled through the narrow neck to the bottom.

Curly-Beard One held a lantern by the hourglass. All the other Curly-Beards leaned over the balcony with their butterfly nets ready. Everything was silent.

Suddenly, Curly-Beard One loudly shouted, "Now!" and the swish of the nets sent a wind whistling over Grandpa Mole's head!

"I caught it! I caught it!" Curly-Beard Five cried out. The strange sound of whirring and flapping shook his net wildly.

The other Tomorrow Catchers rushed to his side. Grandpa Mole stood quietly watching.

In great excitement, the lantern shone upon the shaking net. Two bright eyes stared back. "An owl . . . an owl . . ." all Curly-Beards sighed, in sorrowful tones. "Tomorrow has eluded us again."

In a leather book they marked the 365,233 times the long line of Tomorrow Catchers had failed to catch tomoroow.

In single file they went down the stairs. "Good Night," Grandpa Mole said softly, as he opened the door to the cushion room.

The next morning, Cousin Moles woke up before Grandpa Mole. They tickled him till he woke up laughing.

"It's tomorrow," they shouted.

"No, it's today," Grandpa Mole chuckled. And before they could ask him why they never saw the Tomorrow Catchers at work, he told them all about the happenings at midnight.

For breakfast they had the same food as the night before: bread, water and fruit.

The Tomorrow Catchers were already studying their old, old books when the moles stepped into the great hall. Grandpa Mole sat down by the *Today Book*, and Cousin Moles stood around him.

"Good Morning," the moles said, with smiling voices.

The Tomorrow Catchers looked up with weary faces.

"We are very tired today . . . very tired," they said. "You must realise how wearing it is, staying up late each night in the hope of catching Tomorrow."

"Why do you keep trying?" asked Grandpa Mole. "What benefits will there be?"

"Ah . . . to catch Tomorrow would give us untold benefits. Caught in the safety of our net, we could face Tomorrow. It would be in our hands. We would have no fear of Tomorrow then," Curly-Beard Five spoke longingly.

"You do not count Tomorrow as a friend, then?" Grandpa Mole questioned him.

"No! We must beware of Tomorrow. And be on our guard. And anticipate its demands and schemes. The Tomorrow Catchers spoke all at once, in trembling voices.

"Gentlemen, I have here the *Today Book* . . . brought as a gift for you," Grandpa Mole told them kindly.

"A gift! . . . for us?" The Curly-Beards stood up in surprise, and shuffled to Grandpa Mole's end of the table. "No one has ever brought us a gift before."

Grandpa Mole opened the *Today Book* and began to read: "Surely *goodness* and *mercy* shall follow me all the *days* of my life . . . So teach us to number our *days* . . . Every *day* will I bless Thee . . . This is the *day* that the *Lord* has made, and we will rejoice and be glad in it!"

"That big book is all about Today?" asked the astonished Tomorrow Catchers.

"Every page," smiled Grandpa Mole. "Thousands of wise sayings, all about Today: and most of them from the Lord's own Great Book."

"What does He say about Tomorrow in His Great Book?" all the Curly-Beards wanted to know.

"It is the *Lord* who holds tomorrow! That's why you cannot catch it. But He has given you Today, a moment at a time, in your own hand. His hand reaches out to you each day. And if you will hear His voice, it must be *Today*! That is why the *Today Book* is so precious, and why we brought it as a gift for you."

Grandpa Mole handed the *Today Book* to the Tomorrow Catchers, and they sat down with the book between them, looking at each other.

"Today comes with the Lord's best upon it. Take it as your friend; live with it; laugh with it; love with it; then you'll have no fear of tomorrow."

As Cousin Moles stood listening, they grinned till you could hardly see their eyes. They were so proud of Grandpa Mole!

Yes, they had really been in the Tomorrow Catchers' Castle . . . and they had seen the great butterfly nets . . . and they knew about the fine hourglass . . . and the owl . . . and best of all, they had seen the Tomorrow Catchers carefully studying the *Today Book* as the castle door closed behind them.

Off to the balloon they skipped and ran. "Hurray! we're going back to Dandelion Sea Today!" they shouted.

"Hurray! for Today!" chuckled Grandpa Mole, as the balloon wheezed, "Cushaw! Cushaw!" and took them sailing home.

NOTHING IS IMPOSSIBLE WITH GOD!

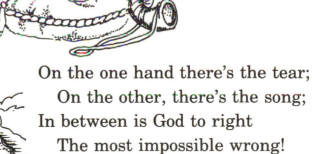

Nothing is impossible,
Nothing is impossible,
Nothing is impossible with God!

On the one hand there's the seed;
    On the other, there's the tree!
In between is God to do
    What's impossible for me!

On the one hand there's the hill;
    On the other, there's the way!
In between is God to do
    What isn't possible, they say!

On the one hand there's the tear;
    On the other, there's the song;
In between is God to right
    The most impossible wrong!

On the one hand there's the boy;
    On the other, there's the king!
In between is God to do
    The most impossible thing!

Nothing is impossible,
Nothing is impossible,
Nothing is impossible with God!

A LETTER TO JESUS

My Very Dearest Jesus,
   It's the ending of the day;
Dad and Mommy kissed me,
   And they listened to me pray.
I'm looking at the stars,
   And they're wide awake like me;
They made me think of You one night
   Beneath an olive tree.
It's hard for me to go asleep,
   So I want You to know
I wish I had been there with You
   Those many years ago.

You see, You needed someone
   Who would stay awake with You;
But all the grown-ups fell asleep,
   As grown-ups often do.
So I would like to tell You,
   That tonight while I'm awake,
If there's a special reason
   In Your heart, that makes it ache,
I'm very wide awake, Lord,
   Just as wide awake can be!
And if You need someone tonight,
   Dear Jesus, please use *me!*

TOGETHER IN THE MEADOW

I was walking all alone,
  Just little me,
Over in the meadow
  And what did I see?

Two little beetles
  In a sheaf together;
Three little frogs
  On a leaf together;
Four little turtles
  On a mound together;
Five little lambs
  Running 'round together;
Six little bugs
  On a frond together;
Seven little ducks
  In a pond together;
Eight little bluebirds
  On a rod together;
Nine little children
  Praising God together!

I joined the little nine,
  So that I made ten;
Then no one in the meadow
  Was alone! Amen!

INDEX